DOVER
CHILDREN'S THRIFT CLASSICS

Tom Sawyer

MARK TWAIN

Adapted by Bob Blaisdell
Illustrated by John Green

DOVER PUBLICATIONS, INC.
Mineola, New York

DOVER CHILDREN'S THRIFT CLASSICS

Published in Canada by General Publishing Company, Ltd., 30 Lesmill Road, Don Mills, Toronto, Ontario.

Published in the United Kingdom by Constable and Company, Ltd., 3 The Lanchesters, 162–164 Fulham Palace Road, London W6 9ER.

Bibliographical Note

This Dover edition, first published in 1996, is a new abridgment by Bob Blaisdell of *The Adventures of Tom Sawyer* (original publication: American Publishing Company, Hartford, 1876). The illustrations by John Green and the introductory Note have been specially prepared for this edition.

Library of Congress Cataloging-in-Publication Data

Twain, Mark, 1835–1910.
    [Adventures of Tom Sawyer]
    Tom Sawyer / Mark Twain ; abridged [by Bob Blaisdell] ; illustrated by John Green.
        p.   cm. — (Dover children's thrift classics)
    "This Dover edition, first published in 1996, is a new abridgement by Bob Blaisdell of The adventures of Tom Sawyer"—T.p. verso.
    Summary: The adventures of a mischievous young boy and his friends, growing up in a Mississippi River town in the nineteenth century.
    ISBN 0-486-29156-1 (pbk.)
    [1. Mississippi River—Fiction.   2. Missouri—Fiction.]   I. Blaisdell, Robert.   II. Green, John, 1948–   ill.   III. Title.   IV. Series.
PZ7.C584Ad   1996
[Fic]—dc20   95-40294
                                                                            CIP
                                                                            AC

Manufactured in the United States of America
Dover Publications, Inc., 31 East 2nd Street, Mineola, N.Y. 11501

Note

THE CHARACTER Tom Sawyer is a creation of the master storyteller and humorist Mark Twain, who also gave us "The Celebrated Jumping Frog of Calaveras County," *The Adventures of Huckleberry Finn* and *A Connecticut Yankee in King Arthur's Court*, as well as many other books. Twain was born Samuel Langhorne Clemens in 1835, and grew up in Hannibal, Missouri, a frontier town on the Mississippi River. His frontier youth, diverse job experience (newspaper writer, steamboat pilot) and wide travels all provided material for his many novels and short stories, which express the spirit of the American West in all its moods. When *The Adventures of Tom Sawyer* was published in 1876, Twain was already one of America's most beloved authors.

This book takes place in the sleepy Missouri town of St. Petersburg, where Tom Sawyer lives with his old Aunt Polly, prowls with his comrade Huckleberry Finn and meets his sweetheart Becky Thatcher. Tom, who is a curious mixture of innocence and mischief, heroism and laziness, is soon pulled into a series of romantic and dangerous adventures having to do with piracy, tedious chores and the cutthroat Injun Joe.

Mark Twain died in 1910, leaving the world a bounty of exuberant, witty prose which it will probably never tire of. This abridged version of his classic novel, which contains the chief nuggets of Tom Sawyer's adventures, will surely leave young readers greedy for more, of which, fortunately, there is plenty.

Contents

Tom Whitewashes a Fence

"TOM!"

No answer.

"Tom!"

No answer.

"What's wrong with that boy, I wonder? You, TOM!"

No answer. The old lady pulled her spectacles down and looked over them about the room.

"Well, if I get hold of you I'll—"

She did not finish, for by this time she was bending down and punching under the bed with the broom.

"I never did see the likes of that boy!"

She went to the open door and stood in it and looked out among the tomato vines and weeds that made up her garden. No Tom. So she lifted her voice and shouted:

"Y-o-u-u, Tom!"

There was a slight noise behind her and she turned just in time to seize a small boy by the slack of his jacket and stop his flight.

"There! I might 'a' thought of that closet. What you been doing in there?"

"Nothing."

"Nothing! Look at your hands. And look at your mouth. What *is* that business?"

Aunt Polly seized Tom by his jacket.

"*I* don't know, aunt."

"Well, I know. It's jam—that's what it is. Forty times I've said if you didn't let that jam alone I'd skin you. Hand me that switch."

The switch hovered in the air above the boy—the peril was near—

"My! Look behind you, aunt!"

The old lady whirled round, and snatched her skirts out of danger. The lad fled, instantly, scrambled up the high board fence, and disappeared over it.

His aunt Polly stood surprised a moment, and then broke into a gentle laugh.

"Hang the boy, can't I never learn anything? Ain't

he played me tricks enough like that for me to be looking out for him by this time? But my goodness, he never plays them alike, two days, and how is a body to know what's coming? He 'pears to know just how long he can torment me before I get my dander up, and he knows if he can make out to put me off for a minute or make me laugh, it's all down again and I can't hit him a lick. I ain't doing my duty by that boy, and that's the Lord's truth, goodness knows. Spare the rod and spile the child, as the Good Book says. But laws! he's my own dead sister's boy, poor thing, and I ain't got the heart to lash him, somehow. He'll play hooky this afternoon, and I'll be obliged to make him work, tomorrow, to punish him. It's mighty hard to make him work Saturdays, when all the boys is having holiday, but he hates work more than he hates anything else."

Tom did play hooky, and he had a very good time. He got back home barely in time to help Jim, a small black boy, saw next day's wood and split the kindlings before supper—at least he was there in time to tell his adventures to Jim while Jim did three-fourths of the work. Tom's younger brother (or rather, half brother), Sid, was already through with his part of the work (picking up wood chips), for he was a quiet boy and had no adventurous, troublesome ways.

When Saturday morning came, all the summer world was bright and fresh, and brimming with life. There was a song in every heart; and if the heart was young the music issued at the lips. There was cheer in every face and a spring in every step.

Jim said he was forbidden to help Tom paint the fence.

Tom appeared on the sidewalk with a bucket of whitewash and a long-handled brush. He surveyed the fence, and all gladness left him and a deep sadness settled down upon his spirit. Thirty yards of board fence nine feet high. Sighing he dipped his brush and passed it along the topmost plank;

repeated the operation; did it again; compared the tiny whitewashed streak with the far-reaching country of the unwhitewashed fence, and sat down on a tree-box discouraged. Jim came skipping out at the gate with a tin pail, and singing. Bringing water from the town pump had always been hateful work in Tom's eyes before, but now it did not strike him so. He remembered that there was company at the pump. White, mulatto, and Negro boys and girls were always there waiting their turns, resting, trading playthings, quarreling, fighting, fooling.

Tom said: "Say, Jim, I'll fetch the water if you'll whitewash some."

Jim shook his head and said: "Can't, Marse Tom. Ole missis, she tole me I got to go an' git dis water an' not stop foolin' round wid anybody. She say she 'spected Marse Tom gwine to ax me to whitewash, an' so she tole me go 'long an' 'tend to my own business—she said *she'd* tend to de whitewashin'."

"Oh, never you mind what she said, Jim. That's the way she always talks. Gimme the bucket—I won't be gone only a minute. *She* won't ever know. I'll give you a white marble! I'll show you my sore toe."

Jim was only human—this attraction was too much for him. He put down his pail, took the marble, and bent over the toe while the bandage was being unwound. In another moment he was flying down the street with his pail and tingling rear, Tom was whitewashing, and Aunt Polly was returning to the house with a slipper in her hand.

But Tom's energy did not last. He began to think of

the fun he had planned for this day, and his sorrows increased. Soon the boys would come tripping along on all sorts of wonderful outings, and they would make a world of fun of him for having to work. And then inspiration burst upon him!

He took up his brush and went calmly to work. Ben Rogers came in sight soon—the very boy, of all boys, whose teasing he had been dreading. Ben was eating an apple, and giving long, cheerful whoops.

Tom went on whitewashing—paid no attention to Ben. The boy stared a moment and then said: "Hi-*yi!* *You're* up a stump, ain't you!"

No answer. Tom looked over his last touch with the eye of an artist, then he gave his brush another gentle sweep and looked over the result, as before. Ben went up alongside of him. Tom's mouth watered for the apple, but he stuck to his work. Ben said, "Hello, old chap, you got to work, hey?"

Tom wheeled suddenly and said, "Why, it's you, Ben! I warn't noticing."

"*Say*—I'm going in a-swimming, *I* am. Don't you wish you could? But of course you'd druther *work*— wouldn't you? Course you would!"

Tom looked at the boy a bit, and said, "What do you call work?"

"Why, ain't *that* work?"

Tom began again his whitewashing, and answered, "Well, maybe it is, and maybe it ain't. All I know is, it suits Tom Sawyer."

"Oh, come now, you don't mean to let on that you *like* it?"

The brush continued to move.

"Like it? Well, I don't see why I oughtn't to like it. Does a boy get a chance to whitewash a fence every day?"

That put the thing in a new light. Ben stopped nibbling his apple. Tom swept his brush daintily back and forth—stepped back to note the effect—added a touch here and there—Ben watching every move and getting more and more interested, more and more pulled in. Soon he said, "Say, Tom, let *me* whitewash a little."

Tom considered, was about to say yes; but he changed his mind: "No—no—I reckon it wouldn't hardly do, Ben. You see, Aunt Polly's awful particular about this fence—right here on the street, you know— but if it was the back fence I wouldn't mind and *she* wouldn't. Yes, she's awful particular about this fence; it's got to be done very careful; I reckon there ain't one boy in a thousand, maybe two thousand that can do it the way it's got to be done."

"No—is that so? Oh, come now—lemme just try. Only just a little—I'd let *you*, if you was me, Tom."

"Ben, I'd like to, honest Injun; but Aunt Polly—well, Jim wanted to do it, but she wouldn't let him; Sid wanted to do it, and she wouldn't let Sid. Now don't you see how I'm fixed? If you was to tackle this fence and anything was to happen to it—"

"Oh, shucks, I'll be just as careful. Now lemme try. Say—I'll give you the core of my apple."

"Well, here— No, Ben, now don't. I'm afeared—"

"I'll give you *all* of it!"

Tom sat on a barrel while the other boys worked.

Tom gave up the brush. While Ben worked and
sweated in the sun, Tom sat on a barrel close by,
dangled his legs, munched his apple, and planned
the trap of more boys. There was no lack of them;
they came to jeer, but remained to whitewash. By the
time Ben was tired out, Tom had traded the next
chance to Billy Fisher for a kite; and when *he* played
out, Johnny Miller bought in for a dead rat and a
string to swing it with—and so on, and so on, hour

after hour. And when the middle of the afternoon
came, Tom was literally rolling in wealth. He had
besides the things before mentioned, twelve marbles,
part of a jew's-harp, a piece of blue bottle glass to
look through, a spool, a key that wouldn't unlock
anything, a piece of chalk, a glass stopper of a bottle,
a tin soldier, a couple of tadpoles, six firecrackers, a
kitten with only one eye, a brass doorknob, a dog
collar—but no dog—the handle of a knife, four pieces
of orange peel, and an old window sash.

He had had a nice, good, idle time all the while—
plenty of company—and the fence had three coats of
whitewash on it! Tom had discovered a great law of
human action, without knowing it—namely, that in

Tom had a kite, twelve marbles, a key and a kitten with one eye.

order to make a man or a boy want a thing, it is only necessary to make the thing difficult to get.

Tom presented himself before Aunt Polly, who was sitting by an open window in a pleasant rear room. The warm summer air, the quiet, and the odor of the flowers had had their effect, and she was napping over her knitting. She had thought that of course Tom had run off long ago, and she was surprised to see him place himself in her power again.

He said, "Mayn't I go and play now, aunt?"

"What, a'ready? How much have you done?"

"It's all done, aunt."

"Tom, don't lie to me—I can't bear it."

"I ain't, aunt; it *is* all done."

Aunt Polly went out to see for herself. She was astonished!

"Well, I never! There's no getting around it, you can work when you're a mind to, Tom.—But it's powerful seldom you're in mind to, I'm bound to say. Well, go 'long and play."

As Tom was passing by the house where Jeff Thatcher lived, he saw a new girl in the garden—a lovely little blue-eyed creature with yellow hair plaited into two long tails, and white summer dress.

He admired this angel without letting on that he was till he saw that she had seen him. Then he pretended he did not know she was there, and began to show off in all sorts of silly boyish ways, in order to win her admiration. He kept up this foolishness for some time; but by and by, while he was in the middle of some dangerous gymnastic stunts, he glanced over and saw that the little girl was making her way toward the house. Tom came up to the fence and leaned on it, hoping she would wait a while longer. She halted a moment on the steps and then moved toward the door. Tom heaved a great sigh as she put her foot on the threshold. But his face lit up right away, for she tossed a pansy over the fence a moment before she disappeared.

2

Tom Meets Becky Thatcher

MONDAY MORNING found Tom Sawyer miserable. Monday mornings always found him so—because it began another week's slow suffering in school. He generally began that day with wishing he had had no holiday, it made the going into prison and chains again so much more hateful.

Tom lay thinking. Soon he thought that he wished he was sick. Here was a possibility. He tried to find a stomach ache, but no, he was fine. Suddenly he discovered something. One of his upper front teeth was loose. This was lucky; he was about to begin to groan as a "starter," as he called it, when it occurred to him that if he told his aunt about it, she would pull it out, and that would hurt. So he thought he would hold the tooth in reserve and look for another trouble. Then he remembered hearing the doctor tell about a thing that laid up a patient for two or three weeks and almost made the patient lose a finger. So the boy drew his sore toe from under the sheet and held it up. He fell to groaning.

But Sid, lying beside him, slept on.

Tom groaned louder, and imagined that he began to feel pain in the toe.

No result from Sid.

Tom was aggravated. He said, "Sid, Sid!" and shook him. Tom began to groan again. Sid yawned, stretched, then brought himself up on his elbow with a snort, and began to stare at Tom. Tom went on groaning.

Sid said, "Tom! Say, Tom!" (No response.) "Here, Tom! *Tom!* What is the matter, Tom?" And he shook him and looked in his face.

Tom moaned out, "Oh, don't, Sid. Don't joggle me."

"Why, what's the matter, Tom? I must call auntie."

"No—never mind. It'll be over by and by, maybe. Don't call anybody."

"But I must! *Don't* groan so, Tom, it's awful. How long you been this way?"

"Hours. Ouch! Oh, don't stir so, Sid, you'll kill me."

"Tom, why didn't you wake me sooner? Oh, Tom, *don't!* What *is* the matter?"

"I forgive you everything, Sid. (Groan.) Everything you've ever done to me. When I'm gone—"

"Oh, Tom, you ain't dying, are you? Don't, Tom— oh, don't. Maybe—"

"I forgive everybody, Sid. (Groan.) Tell 'em so, Sid. And, Sid, you give my window sash and my cat with one eye to that new girl that's come to town, and tell her—"

But Sid had snatched his clothes and gone. He flew downstairs and said, "Oh, Aunt Polly, come! Tom's dying!"

"Dying!"

"Yes'm. Don't wait—come quick!"

"Rubbage! I don't believe it!"

But she fled upstairs with Sid and Mary at her

Aunt Polly gasped, "Tom, what's the matter?"

heels. And her face grew white, too, and her lip trembled. When she reached the bedside she gasped out, "You, Tom! Tom, what's the matter with you?"

"Oh, auntie, I'm—"

"What's the matter with you, child?"

"Oh, auntie, my sore toe's mortified!"

The old lady sank down into a chair and laughed a little, then cried a little, then did both together. "Tom, what a turn you did give me. Now you shut up that nonsense and climb out of this bed."

The groans stopped and the pain disappeared from the toe. The boy felt a little foolish, and he said, "Aunt Polly, it *seemed* mortified, and it hurt so I never minded my tooth at all."

"Your tooth, indeed! What's the matter with your tooth?"

"One of them's loose, and it aches perfectly awful."

"There, there, now, don't begin that groaning again. Open your mouth. Well—your tooth is loose, but you're not going to die about that. Mary, get me a silk thread, and a chunk of hot coal out of the kitchen."

Tom said, "Oh, please, auntie, don't pull it out. It don't hurt any more. I wish I may never stir if it does. Please, don't, auntie. *I* don't want to stay home from school."

"Oh, you don't, don't you? So all this was because you thought you'd get to stay home from school and go a-fishing? Tom, Tom, I love you so, and you seem to try every way you can to break my old heart." By this time the dental instruments were ready. The old lady tied one end of the silk thread to Tom's tooth with a loop and tied the other to the bedpost. Then she seized the chunk of coal and suddenly thrust it almost into the boy's face. The tooth hung dangling by the bedpost now.

But all suffering brings its rewards. As Tom went to school after breakfast, he was the envy of every boy he met because the gap in his upper row of teeth enabled him to spit in a new way. He gathered quite a following of lads interested in this show.

Shortly Tom came upon the young outcast of the

Shortly Tom came upon Huckleberry Finn.

village, Huckleberry Finn, son of the town drunkard.
Huckleberry was hated and dreaded by all the moth-
ers of the town, because he was idle and lawless and

crude and bad—and because all their children admired him so, and delighted in his company, and wished they dared to be like him. Tom was like the rest of the respectable boys, in that he envied Huckleberry and was under strict orders not to play with him. So he played with him every time he got the chance. Huckleberry was always dressed in the cast-off clothes of full-grown men, and they were fluttering and ragged. His hat had a wide crescent torn out of its brim; his coat, when he wore one, hung nearly to his heels and had the rear buttons far down the back; only one suspender supported his pants; the seat of his pants bagged low and contained nothing; the fringed legs dragged in the dirt when not rolled up.

Huckleberry came and went, at his own free will. He slept on doorsteps in fine weather and in empty barrels in wet weather; he did not have to go to school or church, or call anybody master or obey anybody. He could go fishing or swimming when and where he chose, and stay as long as it suited him; nobody forbade him to fight; he could sit up as late as he pleased. He was always the first boy that went barefoot in the spring and the last to put on shoes in the fall. He never had to wash, nor put on clean clothes; he could swear wonderfully. In a word, everything that goes to make life good that boy had. So thought every respectable boy in St. Petersburg.

Tom called out, "Hello, Huckleberry!"

"Hello, yourself, and see how you like it."

"What's that you got?"

"Dead cat."

"Lemme see him, Huck. My, he's pretty stiff. Where'd you get him?"

"Bought him off a boy."

"Say—what is dead cats good for, Huck?"

"Good for? Cure warts with."

"But say—how do you cure 'em with dead cats?"

"Why, you take your cat and go and get in the graveyard 'long about midnight when somebody that was wicked has been buried; and when it's midnight a devil will come, or maybe two or three, but you can't see 'em, you can only hear something like the wind, or maybe hear 'em talk; and when they're taking that fellow away, you heave your cat after 'em and say, 'Devil follow corpse, cat follow devil, warts follow cat, *I*'m done with ye!' That'll fetch *any* wart."

"Sounds right. D'you ever try it, Huck?"

"No, but old Mother Hopkins told me."

"Well, I reckon it's so, then. Say, Hucky, when you going to try the cat?"

"Tonight. I reckon they'll come after old Hoss Williams tonight."

"But they buried him Saturday. Didn't they get him Saturday night?"

"Why, how you talk! How could their charms work till midnight?—and *then* it's Sunday. Devils don't slosh around much of a Sunday, I don't reckon."

"I never thought of that. That's so. Lemme go with you?"

"Of course—if you ain't afeared."

"Afeared! 'Tain't likely. Will you meow?"

"Yes—and you meow back, if you get a chance."

Tom sat down next to the new girl.

When Tom reached the little schoolhouse, he hurried in. He hung his hat on a peg and flung himself into his seat. The teacher, sitting in his armchair, was dozing, but the interruption woke him up. "Thomas Sawyer!"

Tom knew that when his name was pronounced in full, it meant trouble.

"Sir!"

"Come up here. Now, sir, why are you late again, as usual?"

Tom was about to lie, when he saw the girl with the

yellow hair that he had showed off for. And beside this girl was the only vacant space on the girls' side of the schoolhouse. He instantly said, "I STOPPED TO TALK WITH HUCKLEBERRY FINN."

The teacher said, "You—you did what?"

"Stopped to talk with Huckleberry Finn."

"Thomas Sawyer, this is the most astounding confession I have ever listened to. Go and sit with the *girls!* And let this be a warning to you."

He sat down upon the end of the pine bench next to the girl. Soon he began to make secret looks at her. She noticed, "made a mouth" at him and gave him the back of her head for the space of a minute.

When she turned, Tom whispered, "What's your name?"

"Becky Thatcher. What's yours? Oh, I know. It's Thomas Sawyer."

"That's the name they lick me by. I'm Tom when I'm good. You call me Tom, will you?"

When school broke up at noon, Tom whispered in Becky Thatcher's ear:

"Put on your bonnet and let on you're going home; and when you get to the corner give the rest of 'em the slip and turn down through the lane and come back. I'll go the other way and come back."

So the one went off with one group of students, and the other went with another. In a little while the two met at the bottom of the lane, and when they reached the school they had it all to themselves. Then they sat together and fell to talking. Tom was swimming with bliss. He said, "Do you love rats?"

"No! I hate them!"

"Well, I do, too—*live* ones. But I mean dead ones, to swing round your head with a string."

"No, I don't care for rats much, anyway. What *I* like is chewing gum."

"Oh, I should say so. I wish I had some now."

"Do you? I've got some. I'll let you chew it awhile, but you must give it back to me."

That was fine, so they chewed it turn about and dangled their legs against the bench.

3

Adventure in the Graveyard

AT HALF past nine, that night, Tom and Sid were sent to bed, as usual. They said their prayers, and Sid was soon asleep. Tom lay awake and waited. When it seemed to him that it must be nearly daylight, he heard the clock strike ten! So he lay still, and stared up into the dark. By and by, he began to doze, in spite of himself. The clock chimed eleven, but he did not hear it. And then there came, mingling with his dreams, a sad moaning. A minute later, Tom was dressed and out the window and creeping along the roof of the house on all fours. He meowed once or twice as he went, then jumped to the roof of the woodshed and then to the ground. Huckleberry Finn was there, with his dead cat. The boys moved off and disappeared in the gloom. At the end of half an hour they were wading through the tall grass of the graveyard.

It was a graveyard of the old-fashioned western kind. It was on a hill, about a mile and a half from the village. It had a crazy board fence around it, which leaned inward in places, and outward the rest of the time, but stood upright nowhere. Grass and weeds grew over the whole cemetery. All the old graves were

Tom crept along the roof to join Huck Finn.

sunken in, there was not a tombstone on the place; round-topped, worm-eaten boards staggered over the graves, leaning for support and finding none.

A faint wind moaned through the trees, and Tom feared it might be the spirits of the dead, complaining of being disturbed. The boys talked little. They found the new heap of earth they were seeking, and placed themselves within the protection of three great elms that grew in a bunch within a few feet of the grave.

Then they waited in silence for what seemed a long time. Tom said in a whisper, "Hucky, do you believe the dead people like it for us to be here?"

Huckleberry whispered, "I wisht I knowed. It's awful gloomy like, *ain't* it?"

Some figures approached the boys through the gloom.

"I bet it is." Suddenly Tom grabbed his friend's arm and said, "Sh!"

"What is it, Tom?"

"Sh! There 'tis again. Didn't you hear it?"

"Lord, Tom, they're coming! They're coming sure. What'll we do?"

"I don't know. Think they'll see us?"

"Oh, Tom, they can see in the dark, same as cats. I wisht I hadn't come."

A sound of voices floated up from the far end of the graveyard. Some figures approached through the gloom, swinging an old-fashioned tin lantern that freckled the ground with little spangles of light. Huckleberry whispered, "It's the devils, sure enough. Three of 'em! Lordy, Tom, we're goners!—Wait, they're humans! One of 'em's old Muff Potter's voice."

"Say, Huck, I know another o' them voices; it's Injun Joe."

"That's so—that murderin' half-breed! I'd druther they was devils. What kin they be up to?"

The whispering died out now, for the three men had reached the grave and stood within a few feet of the boys' hiding place.

"Here it is," said the third voice; and the owner of it held the lantern up and revealed young Dr. Robinson.

Potter and Injun Joe were carrying a handbarrow with a rope and couple of shovels on it. They cast down their load and began to open the grave. The doctor put the lantern at the head of the grave and came and sat down with his back against one of the elm trees. He was so close the boys could have touched him.

"Hurry, men!" he said. "The moon might come out at any moment."

They growled in response and went on digging.

Finally a spade struck upon the coffin, and within another minute or two the men had pulled it up and out on the ground. They pried off the lid with their shovels, got out the body and dumped it on the ground. The moon came out from behind the clouds and shone on this scene. The corpse was placed on the barrow and covered with a blanket.

"Now the cussed thing's out, Sawbones, and you'll just pay us out another five, or here it stays," said Potter.

"Look here, what does this mean?" said the doctor. "You asked for your pay in advance, and I've paid you."

"Yes, and you done more than that," said Injun Joe, approaching the doctor, who was now standing. "Five years ago, you drove me away from your father's kitchen one night, when I come to ask for something to eat, and you said I warn't there for any good; and when I swore I'd get even with you if it took a hundred years, your father had me jailed for a vagrant. Did you think I'd forget?" He was threatening the doctor, with his fist in his face, by this time. The doctor struck out suddenly and knocked the ruffian to the ground.

"Here, now, don't you hit my pard!" said Potter, dropping his knife. The next moment he had grabbed the doctor and they were struggling. Injun Joe sprang to his feet, his eyes flaming, snatched up Potter's knife, and went round and round the fighters, seeking a chance. All at once the doctor flung himself free, picked up the heavy headboard of Williams' grave

The doctor swung the headboard of the grave.

and knocked Potter down with it—and in the same instant the half-breed saw his chance and drove the knife to the hilt in the young man's breast. The doctor tumbled over and fell partly on Potter, dashing him with his blood. In the same moment the clouds blotted out the scene and the two frightened boys went speeding away in the dark.

Soon, when the moon came out again, Injun Joe was standing over the two men. He robbed the doctor's dead body. After which he put the fatal knife in Potter's open right hand, and sat down on the coffin. Five minutes passed and then Potter began to stir and moan. His hand closed upon the knife; he raised it and glanced at it, and let it fall. Then he sat up, pushing the body from him, and gazed at it, and then around him. His eyes met Joe's.

"Lord, how is this, Joe?" he said.

"It's a dirty business," said Joe. "What did you do it for?"

"I! I never done it!"

"Look here! That kind of talk won't wash."

Potter trembled and grew white. "I thought I'd got sober. I'd no business to drink tonight. But it's in my head yet. I'm all in a muddle; can't recollect anything of it, hardly. Tell me, Joe—*honest*, now, old feller—did I do it? Joe, I never meant to—'pon my soul and honor, I never meant to, Joe. Tell me how it was, Joe. Oh, it's awful—and him so young and promising."

"Why, you two was scuffling, and he fetched you one with the headboard and you fell flat; and then up you come, all reeling and staggering, like, and snatched the knife and jammed it into him, just as he fetched you another awful clip—and here you've laid, as dead as a wedge till now."

"Oh, I didn't know what I was a-doing. I wish I may die this minute if I did. It was all on account of the whisky; and the excitement, I reckon. I never used a weapon in my life before, Joe. Joe, don't tell! Say you won't tell, Joe—that's a good feller. I always liked you and stood up for you, too. Don't you remember? You *won't* tell, *will* you, Joe?" And the poor creature dropped on his knees before the murderer, and clasped his hands.

"No, you've always been fair and square with me, Muff Potter, and I won't go back on you. There, now, that's as fair as a man can say."

"Oh, Joe, you're an angel. I'll bless you for this the longest day I live." And Potter began to cry.

"Come now, that's enough of that. This ain't any time for blubbering. You be off yonder way and I'll go this."

The two boys, meanwhile, had flown on and on, toward the village.

They stopped in the old tannery, panting hard.

"Huckleberry," Tom whispered, "what do you reckon'll come of this?"

"If Dr. Robinson dies, I reckon hanging'll come of it."

"Who'll tell? We?"

"What are you talking about? S'pose something happened and Injun Joe didn't hang? Why he'd kill us some time or other, just as dead sure as we're a-laying here. Now, look-a-here, Tom, let's take and swear to one another—that's what we got to do—swear to keep mum. But there orter be writing 'bout a big thing like this. And blood."

Tom picked up a clean pine shingle that lay in the moonlight, took a fragment of chalk out of his pocket, got the moon on his work, and painfully scrawled these lines:

"Huck Finn and Tom Sawyer swears they will keep mum about this and they wish they may drop down dead in their tracks if they ever tell and rot."

Huckleberry was filled with admiration of Tom's writing, and the grandness of the language. Tom unwound the thread from one of his needles, and each boy pricked the ball of his thumb and squeezed out a drop of blood. In time, after many squeezes, Tom managed to sign his initials, using the ball of his finger for a pen. Then he showed Huckleberry how to make an H and an F, and the oath was complete. They buried the shingle close to the wall.

Then they separated. When Tom crept in at his bedroom window the night was almost gone. He undressed and fell asleep.

Close upon the hour of noon the whole village was suddenly electrified with the ghastly news. A gory knife had been found close to the murdered man, and it had been recognized by somebody as belonging to Muff Potter.

All the town was drifting toward the graveyard, even Huck and Tom. Poor Muff Potter was caught nearby, and his eyes showed the fear that was upon him. When the sheriff brought him to the site, Potter stood before the murdered man, put his face in his hands and burst into tears.

"I didn't do it, friends," he sobbed, "'pon my word and honor I never done it." He saw Injun Joe there, and exclaimed, "Tell 'em, Joe, tell 'em!"

Then Huckleberry and Tom stood dumb and staring and heard the liar reel off his statement that Potter had killed the doctor. Potter was hauled off to jail.

Tom's fearful secret and conscience disturbed his

sleep for as much as a week after this. Every day or two, during this time of sorrow, Tom watched his opportunity and went to the little jail window and smuggled any small comforts through to Potter, the "murderer," as he could get hold of.

4
Life as a Pirate

ONE OF the reasons why Tom's mind finally drifted away from its secret troubles was that it had found a new matter to interest itself about. Becky Thatcher had stopped coming to school. She was ill. What if she should die? The charm of life was gone.

Finally, one morning at school, Becky passed in at the gate, and Tom's heart gave a great bound. The next instant he was "going on"; yelling, laughing, chasing boys, jumping over the fence at risk of life and limb, throwing handsprings, standing on his head—doing all the heroic things he could think of, and keeping an eye out all the while, to see if Becky was noticing. But she never looked. Could it be possible that she was not aware that he was there? He went closer; came war-whooping around, snatched a boy's cap, hurled it to the roof of the schoolhouse, broke through a group of boys, tumbling them in every direction, and fell sprawling, himself, under Becky's nose, almost upsetting her—and she turned, with her nose in the air, and he heard her say: "Mf! some people think they're smart—always showing off!"

Tom's mind was made up now. He was gloomy. He

Tom did handsprings, watching to see if Becky noticed.

was a forsaken, friendless boy, he said; nobody loved him; when they found out what they had driven him to, perhaps they would be sorry; he had tried to do right and get along, but they would not let him; since nothing would do them but to be rid of him, let it be so.

By this time he was far down Meadow Lane, away from school. Just at this point he met his soul's sworn comrade, Joe Harper. Tom, wiping his eyes with his sleeve, began to blubber out something about escaping from hard usage and lack of sympathy at home by roaming abroad into the great world never to return.

Jackson's Island.

It happened that Joe had come to Tom to declare such a thing himself. Joe's mother had whipped him for drinking some cream; it was plain that she was tired of him and wished him to go. If she felt that way, there was nothing for him to do but give in; he hoped she would be happy, and never regret having driven her poor boy out into the unfeeling world to suffer and die.

As the two boys walked along, they made a deal to stand by each other and be brothers and never separate till death. Then they began to lay their plans. Joe was for being a hermit, and living on crusts of bread in a remote cave; but after listening to Tom, he agreed that there were some advantages about a life of crime, and so he went along with becoming a pirate.

Three miles below St. Petersburg, at a point where the Mississippi River was a trifle over a mile wide, there was a long, narrow, wooded island. No one lived there; it lay far over toward the farther shore, near a dense forest. So Jackson's Island was chosen. Who were to be the subjects of their piracies was a matter that did not occur to them. Then they hunted Huckleberry Finn, and he joined them, for all careers were one to him. They separated to meet at a lonely spot two miles above the village at the favorite hour— which was midnight. There was a small log raft there which they meant to capture. Each would bring hooks and lines, and such food as he could steal.

About midnight Tom arrived with a boiled ham and stopped on a small bluff overlooking the meeting place. It was starlight and very still. The mighty river lay like an ocean at rest. Tom gave a low whistle. It was answered from under the bluff.

"Who goes there?"

"Tom Sawyer, the Black Avenger of the Spanish Main. Name your names."

"Huck Finn the Red-Handed, and Joe Harper the Terror of the Seas." Tom had given them these titles, from his favorite books.

Then Tom tumbled his ham over the bluff and let himself down after it.

The Terror of the Seas had brought a side of bacon. Finn the Red-Handed had stolen a skillet and a lot of tobacco, and had also brought a few corncobs to make pipes with. The Black Avenger of the Spanish Main said it would never do to start without some fire. Matches were hardly known there in that day. They saw a fire smoldering upon a great raft a hundred yards above, and they sneaked there and helped themselves to a chunk.

The raft drew beyond the middle of the river.

They shoved off, soon after, Tom in command, Huck at the after oar and Joe at the forward. The raft drew beyond the middle of the river; the boys pointed her head right and then lay on their oars. The river was not high, so there was not more than a two- or three-mile current. Hardly a word was said during the next three-quarters of an hour. Now the raft was passing before the distant town. Two or three glimmering lights showed where it lay.

About two o'clock in the morning the raft grounded on a sand bar two hundred yards above the head of Jackson's Island, and they waded back and forth until they had moved their cargo onto the island.

They built a fire against the side of a great log twenty or thirty steps within the dark depths of the forest, and then cooked up some bacon in the frying pan for supper, and used up half of the corn pone stock they had brought. It seemed glorious to be feasting on that uninhabited island, far from the haunts of men, and they said they would never return to civilization.

"Ain't it great?" said Joe.

"It's the best," said Tom. "What would the boys say if they could see us?"

"Say? Well, they'd just die to be here—hey, Hucky!"

"I reckon so," said Huckleberry. "Anyways, *I'm* suited. I don't want nothing better'n this."

"It's just the life for me," said Tom. "You don't have to get up, mornings, and you don't have to go to school, and wash, and all that blame foolishness. You see a pirate don't have to do *anything*, Joe, when he's ashore, but a hermit *he* has to be praying considerable, and then he don't have any fun, anyway, all by himself that way."

"Oh, yes, that's so," said Joe. "But I hadn't thought much about it, you know. I'd a good deal rather be a pirate, now that I've tried it."

Gradually their talk died out and sleepiness began to steal upon them. Huck fell asleep easily, but Joe and Tom began to feel a fear that they had been doing wrong to run away. And next they thought of the stolen meat. They decided that so long as they remained in the pirate business, their piracies should not again involve the crime of stealing. Now they fell peacefully to sleep.

When Tom awoke in the morning, he wondered

where he was. He sat up and rubbed his eyes and looked around. Then he remembered. It was the cool gray dawn, and there was a beautiful feeling of peace in the woods. Tom stirred up the other pirates, and in a minute or two they were stripped and chasing after and tumbling over each other in the shallow water of the white sand bar. They felt no longing for the little village sleeping in the distance beyond the river. A current or rise in the river had carried off their raft, but they were pleased, since its going was something like burning the bridge between them and civilization.

They came back to camp and soon had the campfire blazing up again. Huck found a spring of clear cold water close by, and the boys made cups of oak or hickory leaves and felt that water would be a good enough substitute for coffee. While Joe was slicing bacon for breakfast, Tom and Huck asked him to hold on a minute; they stepped to a promising nook in the riverbank and threw in their lines; almost immediately they had their reward. They came back with some handsome bass, a couple of sun perch, and a small catfish. They fried the fish with the bacon, and were astonished, for no fish had ever seemed so delicious before.

They lay around in the shade, after breakfast, while Huck had a smoke, and then went off through the woods on an exploring expedition. They found plenty of things to be delighted with. They discovered that the island was about three miles long and a quarter of a mile wide, and that the shore it lay closest to was only separated from it by a narrow channel hardly

The boys could not figure out what the ferryboat was doing.

two hundred yards wide. They took a swim every hour, so it was close to the middle of the afternoon when they got back to camp. They were too hungry to stop to fish, but they ate well upon cold ham and then threw themselves down in the shade to talk. The stillness of the woods and the sense of loneliness began to affect the spirits of the boys. They fell to thinking. A longing crept upon them—it was budding homesickness. Even Finn the Red-Handed was dreaming of his doorsteps and empty barrels. But they were all ashamed to speak of their missing home.

The boys began to notice a strange sound in the distance. There was a long silence, then a deep boom came floating down out of the distance.

" 'Tain't thunder," said Huckleberry.

They sprang to their feet and hurried to the shore toward the town. They parted the bushes on the bank and peered out over the water. The little steam ferryboat was about a mile below the village, drifting with the current. Her broad deck seemed crowded with people. There were a great many rowboats in the neighborhood of the ferryboat, but the boys could not figure out what the men in them were doing. Soon a great jet of white smoke burst from the ferryboat's side, and as it expanded and rose in a lazy cloud, that same dull boom came to the listeners again.

"I know now!" exclaimed Tom. "Somebody's drownded!"

"That's it!" said Huck. "They done that last summer, when Bill Turner got drownded; they shoot a cannon over the water, and that makes him come up to the top. Yes, and they take loaves of bread and put quicksilver in 'em and set 'em afloat, and wherever there's anybody that's drownded, they'll float right there and stop."

"By jings, I wish I was over there, now," said Joe.

"I do too," said Huck. "I'd give heaps to know who it is."

"Boys," said Tom, "I know who's drownded—it's us!"

They felt like heroes in an instant. Here was a great triumph; they were missed; they were mourned; hearts were breaking; and best of all, the dead boys were the talk of the whole town, and the envy of all the boys. This was fine. It was worth while to be a pirate.

As twilight drew on, the ferryboat went back and

the rowboats disappeared. The pirates returned to their camp. They were jubilant with their new fame and the great trouble they were making. They caught fish, cooked supper and ate, and then fell to guessing at what the village was thinking and saying about them. But when the shadows of night closed them in, they gradually stopped talking, and sat gazing into the fire. The excitement was gone now, and Tom and Joe could not keep back thoughts of certain persons at home who were not enjoying this fine frolic as much as they were. They grew troubled and unhappy; a sigh or two escaped.

As the night deepened, Huck began to nod, and soon to snore. Joe followed next. Tom lay upon his elbow for some time, watching the two. At last he got up. Then he tiptoed his way among the trees till he felt that he was out of hearing, and broke into a keen run in the direction of the sand bar.

A few minutes later Tom was wading toward the shore. Before the depth reached his middle he was halfway over; the current would permit no more wading, now, so he swam the remaining hundred yards. He went through the woods, following the shore. Shortly before ten o'clock he came out into an open place near the village. He flew along alleys, and shortly found himself at his aunt's back fence. He climbed over and looked in at the sitting-room window, for a light was burning there. There sat Aunt Polly, Sid, Mary, and Joe Harper's mother, grouped together, talking. They were by the bed, and the bed was between them and the door. Tom went to the

Tom looked in at the sitting-room window.

door and began to softly lift the latch; then he pressed gently, and the door yielded a crack; he continued pushing, and quaking every time it creaked, till he judged he might squeeze through on his knees.

"What makes the candle blow so?" said Aunt Polly. "Why, that door's open, I believe. Go 'long and shut it, Sid."

Tom disappeared under the bed just in time. He then crept to where he could almost touch his aunt's foot.

"But as I was saying," said Aunt Polly, "he warn't *bad,* so to say—only misch*ee*vous. Only just giddy, and harum-scarum, you know. He warn't any more responsible than a colt. *He* never meant any harm, and he was the best-hearted boy that ever was"—and she began to cry.

"It was just so with my Joe—always full of his devilment and up to every kind of mischief, but he was just as unselfish and kind as he could be—and laws bless me, to think I went and whipped him for taking that cream, never once recollecting that I throwed it out myself because it was sour, and I never to see him again in this world!" And Mrs. Harper sobbed as if her heart would break.

"Oh, Mrs. Harper," said Aunt Polly, "I don't know how to give him up! I don't know how to give him up! He was such a comfort to me, although he tormented my old heart out of me, 'most. But he's out of all his troubles now—"

This was too much for the old lady, and she broke entirely down. Tom was snuffling, now, himself—and more in pity of himself than anybody else. He went on listening, and gathered by odds and ends that it was thought the boys had been drowned mid-channel, since the boys, being good swimmers, would otherwise have escaped to shore. This was Wednesday night. If the bodies continued missing until Sunday, all hope would be given over and the funerals would be preached on that morning.

Mrs. Harper gave a sobbing goodnight and turned to go. Then the two bereaved women flung themselves into each other's arms and had a good cry, and then parted.

Aunt Polly knelt down and prayed for Tom so touchingly, so appealingly, and with such measureless love in her words and her old trembling voice, that he was in tears long before she was through.

He had to keep still long after she went to bed, for she kept making brokenhearted sighs from time to time. But at last she was still, only moaning a little in her sleep. Now the boy stole out, rose gradually by her bedside, and stood regarding her. His heart was full of pity for her. He bent over and kissed her lips, and right away made his exit, latching the door behind him.

He threaded his way back to the shore opposite the island and swam across and returned to the pirate camp.

For the next couple of days they hunted and played and swam and ran a circus starring three clowns. But by Friday, they were all so homesick they could hardly endure the misery of it.

Joe said, "Oh, boys, let's give it up. I want to go home. It's so lonesome."

"Oh, no, Joe, you'll feel better by and by," said Tom. "Just think of the fishing that's here."

"I don't care for fishing, I want to go home."

"But, Joe, there ain't such another swimming place anywhere."

"Swimming's no good. I don't seem to care for it, somehow, when there ain't anybody to say I shan't go in. I mean to go home."

"Oh, shucks! Baby! You want to see your mother, I reckon."

"Yes, I do want to see my mother—and you would, too, if you had one. I ain't any more baby than you are." And Joe snuffled a little.

"Well, we'll let the crybaby go home to his mother, *won't* we, Huck? *You* like it here, don't you, Huck? We'll stay, won't we?"

Huck said "Y-e-s"—but without any heart in it.

"Go 'long home, Joe," said Tom, "and get laughed at. Oh, you're a nice pirate. Huck and me ain't no crybabies. We'll stay, won't we, Huck?"

Huck now said, "I want to go, too, Tom. It was getting so lonesome anyway, and now it'll be worse. Let's us go, too, Tom."

"I won't! You can all go, if you want to. I mean to stay."

"Tom, I wisht you'd come too. Now you think it over. We'll wait for you when we get to shore."

"Well, you'll wait a blame long time, that's all."

Huck started away, and Tom stood looking after him. He hoped the boys would stop, but they still waded slowly on.

He darted after his comrades, yelling, "Wait! Wait! I want to tell you something!"

They stopped and turned around. When he got to

where they were, he began unfolding his secret, and they listened till at last they saw the point he was driving at, and then they set up a war whoop of applause and said it was "splendid!" and said if he had told them at first they wouldn't have started away.

The lads came merrily back and went at their sports again with a will, chattering all the time about Tom's stupendous plan and admiring the genius of it. The next day, Saturday, the boys played Indians all afternoon.

When the Sunday-school hour was finished, the next morning, the bell began to toll, instead of ringing in the usual way. It was a very quiet Sunday. The villagers began to gather, pausing a moment outside the church to whisper about the sad event. But there was no whispering in the church. None could remember when the little church had been so full before. When Aunt Polly entered, followed by Sid and Mary, and the Harper family, all in deep black, the congregation rose and stood until the mourners were seated in the front pew.

Then the minister prayed. A moving hymn was sung, and then the sermon followed.

As the service proceeded, the clergyman drew such pictures of the qualities, the winning ways, and the great promise of the lost lads that every soul there, thinking he recognized those pictures, felt a pang in remembering that he had seen only faults and flaws in the poor boys. The minister related many a touching event in the lives of the departed, too, which

Tom led the march up the aisle.

illustrated their sweet, generous natures, and the people could easily see, now, how noble and beautiful those times were. The congregation became more and more moved, as the sad tale went on, till at last the whole company broke down and joined the weeping mourners in a chorus of sobs, the preacher himself giving way to his feelings and crying in the pulpit.

There was a rustle in the gallery, which nobody noticed; a moment later the church door creaked; the minister raised his streaming eyes above his handkerchief, and stood transfixed! First one and then another pair of eyes followed the minister's, and then almost as one the congregation rose and stared while the three dead boys came marching up the aisle, Tom in the lead, Joe next, and Huck in the rear! They had been hid in the unused gallery listening to their own funeral sermon!

Aunt Polly, Mary, and the Harpers threw themselves upon their restored ones, smothered them with kisses, while poor Huck stood uncomfortable, not knowing exactly what to do or where to hide from so many eyes. He started to slink away, but Tom seized him and said: "Aunt Polly, it ain't fair. Somebody's got to be glad to see Huck."

"And so they shall. I'm glad to see him, poor motherless thing!"

Suddenly the minister shouted at the top of his voice: "Praise God for whom all blessings flow— SING!—and put your hearts in it!"

And they did. While the hymn shook the rafters, Tom Sawyer the Pirate looked around him and confessed in his heart that this was the proudest moment of his life.

Tom got more knocks and kisses that day—according to Aunt Polly's moods—than he had earned before in a year.

What a hero about the village Tom was become, now! He did not go skipping and prancing, but moved with the swagger of a pirate. Smaller boys than himself flocked at his heels, as proud to be seen with him as if he had been the drummer at the head of a parade. Boys of his own size pretended not to know he had been away at all; but they were envious. They would have given anything to have Tom's fame. At school the children made so much of him and of Joe that the two heroes were not long in becoming stuck up.

5

Muff Potter's Trial

VACATION CAME. Becky Thatcher, who had been overjoyed to see Tom again after his "drowning," was gone to her home to stay with her parents during vacation—so there was no bright side to life anywhere for Tom.

The dreadful secret of the murder was a terrible misery. The murder trial came on in the court. It became the talk of the village immediately and Tom could not get away from it. Every reference to the murder sent a shudder to his heart. This gossip kept him in a cold shiver all the time, and so he took Huck to a lonely place to have a talk with him. It would be some relief to unseal his tongue for a little while.

"Huck, have you told anybody about—that?"

" 'Bout what?"

"You know what."

"Oh—course I haven't."

"Never a word?"

"Never a solitary word, so help me. We wouldn't be alive two days if that got found out. *You* know that."

"Huck, they couldn't anybody get you to tell, could they?"

"Get me to tell? Why, if I wanted that half-breed

50

devil to drownd me they could get me to tell. They ain't no different way."

"Well, that's all right, then," said Tom. "I reckon we're safe as long as we keep mum."

"But the talk's just Muff Potter, Muff Potter, Muff Potter all the time. It keeps me in a sweat."

"That's just the same way they go round me. I reckon he's a goner. Don't you feel sorry for him, sometimes?"

"Most always—most always," said Huck. "He hain't ever done anything to hurt anybody. Just fishes a little, to get money to get drunk on—and loafs around considerable; but, Lord, we all do that—leastways most of us. But he's kind of good—he gave me half a fish, once, when there wasn't enough for two; and lots of times he's kind of stood by me when I was out of luck."

"Well, he's mended kites for me, Huck, and knitted hooks onto my line. I wish we could get him out of there."

"My! we couldn't get him out, Tom. And besides, 'twouldn't do any good; they'd ketch him again."

The boys had a long talk, but it brought them little comfort. They did as they had often done before— went to the cell grating and gave Potter some tobacco and matches. He was on the ground floor and there were no guards.

His gratitude for their gifts had always made them feel guilty—it cut deeper than ever this time, when Potter said: "You've been mighty good to me, boys— better'n anybody else in this town. And I don't forget

Huck and Tom often went to the cell to visit Potter.

it, I don't. Well, boys, I done an awful thing—drunk and crazy at the time—that's the only way I account for it—and now I got to swing for it, and it's right. Right, and best, too, I reckon—hope so, anyway. Well, we won't talk about that. I don't want to make *you* feel bad."

Tom went home miserable, and his dream that night was full of horrors. The next day and the day after, he hung about the courtroom, drawn to go in, but forcing himself to stay out. Huck was having the same experience. At the end of the second day the village talk was to the effect that Injun Joe's evidence stood firm and unshaken, and that there was not the slightest question as to what the jury's verdict would be.

Tom was out late that night, doing something, and came to bed through the window. He was in a tremendous state of excitement. It was hours before he got to sleep. All the village flocked to the courthouse the next morning, for this was to be the great day. After a long wait the jury filed in and took their places; shortly afterward, Potter, pale and haggard, timid and hopeless, was brought in, with chains upon him, and seated where all the curious eyes could stare at him; no less conspicuous was Injun Joe, quiet as ever. There was another pause, and then the judge arrived and the sheriff proclaimed the opening of the court.

Now a witness was called who testified that he found Muff Potter washing in the brook, at an early hour of the morning that the murder was discovered, and that he immediately sneaked away. After some further questioning, counsel for the prosecution said:

"Take the witness."

The prisoner raised his eyes for a moment, but dropped them again when his own counsel said, "I have no questions to ask him."

The next witness proved the finding of the knife near the corpse. Counsel for the prosecution said, "Take the witness."

"I have no questions to ask him," Potter's lawyer replied.

A third witness swore he had often seen the knife in Potter's possession.

"Take the witness."

Counsel for Potter declined to question him. The faces of the audience began to show annoyance. Did this attorney mean to throw away his client's life without an effort?

Several witnesses talked about Potter's guilty behavior when brought to the scene of the murder. They were allowed to leave the stand without being cross-examined.

Every detail of what occurred in the graveyard upon that morning was brought out by believable witnesses, but none of them were cross-examined by Potter's lawyer.

The prosecution now said, "By the oaths of citizens whose simple word is above suspicion, we have fastened this awful crime, beyond all possibility of question, upon the unhappy prisoner. We rest our case."

A groan escaped from poor Potter, and he put his face in his hands and rocked his body softly to and fro, while a painful silence came over the courtroom. Many men were moved, and many women cried. Counsel for the defense rose and said, "Your honor, in our remarks at the opening of this trial, we gave

Tom took his place upon the witness stand.

our purpose as proving that our client did this fearful deed while under the influence of too much alcohol. We have changed our mind. We shall not offer that plea." He turned to the clerk and said, "Call Thomas Sawyer!"

A puzzled amazement awoke in every face in the house, not even excepting Potter's. The boy was very scared as he rose and took his place upon the stand.

"Thomas Sawyer, where were you on the seventeenth of June, about the hour of midnight?"

Tom glanced at Injun Joe's iron face and his tongue stopped. The audience listened breathless, but the words refused to come. After a few moments, however, the boy got a little of his strength back, and said: "In the graveyard!"

"A little louder, please. Don't be afraid. You were—"

"In the graveyard."

A savage smile went across Injun Joe's face.

"Were you anywhere near Horse Williams's grave?"

"Yes, sir."

"Speak up—just a trifle louder. How near were you?"

"Near as I am to you."

"Were you hidden, or not?"

"I was hid."

"Where?"

"Behind the elms that's on the edge of the grave."

Injun Joe gave a start.

"Anyone with you?"

"Yes, sir, I went there with—"

"Wait—wait a moment. Never mind mentioning your companion's name. We will bring him up to the stand at the proper time. Did you carry anything there with you?"

Tom hesitated and looked confused.

"Speak out, my boy—don't be shy. The truth is always respectable. What did you take there?"

"Only a—a—dead cat."

There was laughter, which the court officers stopped.

"We will produce the skeleton of that cat. Now, my boy, tell us everything that occurred—tell it in your own way—don't skip anything, and don't be afraid."

Tom began—hesitatingly at first, but as he warmed

Injun Joe tore through the crowd and was gone.

to his subject his words flowed more and more easily; in a little while every sound stopped but his own voice; every eye fixed itself upon him; with parted lips and held breath the audience hung upon his words, taking no note of time, fascinated by the tale. The climax came when the boy said, "—and the doctor fetched the board around and Muff Potter fell, Injun Joe jumped with the knife and—"

Crash! Quick as lightning the half-breed sprang for a window, tore his way through all opposers, and was gone!

Tom was a glittering hero once more—the pet of the old, the envy of the young. His name even went into print, for the village paper wrote about him. The village took Muff Potter to its bosom now.

6
Hunting for Treasure

TOM'S DAYS were days of splendor, but his nights were seasons of horror. Injun Joe was in all his dreams, and always with doom in his eye. Poor Huck was in the same state of terror, for Tom had told the whole story to the lawyer the night before the great day of the trial, and Huck was sore afraid that his share in the business might come out too.

Every day Muff Potter's gratitude made Tom glad he had spoken; but nightly he wished he had sealed up his tongue. Half the time Tom was afraid Injun Joe would never be captured; the other half he was afraid he would be. He felt sure he never could draw a safe breath again until that man was dead and he had seen the corpse.

Rewards had been offered, the country had been looked over, but no Injun Joe was found.

The slow days of summer drifted on, and each left behind a slightly lightened weight of fear on Tom.

There comes a time in every boy's life when he has a raging desire to go somewhere and dig for hidden treasure. This desire came upon Tom one day. He stumbled upon Huck, and told Huck about it, and Huck was willing.

"Where'll we dig?" he asked.

"Oh," said Tom, "most anywhere."

"Why, is it hid all around?"

"No, indeed it ain't. It's hid in mighty particular places, Huck—sometimes on islands, sometimes in rotten chests under the end of a limb of an old dead tree, just where the shadow falls at midnight; but mostly under the floor in haunted houses."

"Who hides it?"

"Why, robbers, of course—who'd you reckon?"

"I don't know. If 'twas mine I wouldn't hide it; I'd spend it and have a good time."

"So would I. But robbers don't do that way. They always hide it and leave it there."

"Don't they come after it any more?"

"No, they think they will, but they generally forget the marks, or else they die. Anyway, it lays there a long time and gets rusty. There's the old haunted house up the Still-House branch, and there's lots of dead-limb trees."

"Is it under all of them?"

"How you talk! No!"

"Then how you going to know which one to go for?"

"Go for all of 'em!"

"Why, Tom, that'll take all summer."

"Well, what of that? S'pose we tackle that old dead-limb tree on the hill t'other side of Still-House branch?"

"I'm agreed."

So they got a pick and a shovel, and set out on their three-mile tramp.

"Say, Huck, if we find a treasure here, what you going to do with your share?"

"Well, I'll have pie and a glass of soda every day, and I'll go to every circus that comes along. What you going to do with yourn, Tom?"

"I'm going to buy a new drum, and a sword, and a red necktie and a bull pup, and get married."

"Married!"

"That's it."

"Tom, you—why, you ain't in your right mind."

"Anyway, let's go to digging."

They worked and sweated for half an hour. No result. They toiled another half hour without result. Huck said, "Do they always bury it as deep as this?"

"Sometimes—not always. Not generally. I reckon we haven't got the right place."

So they chose a new spot and began again. By and by Huck said, "Blame it, we must be in the wrong place again."

"It is mighty curious, Huck. I don't understand it.— Oh, I know what the matter is! What a blamed lot of fools we are! You got to find out where the shadow of the limb falls at midnight, and that's where you dig!"

"Then consound it, we've fooled away all this work for nothing. Well, I'll come around and meow tonight."

"All right."

The boys were there that night, about the appointed time. They marked where the shadow fell, and began to dig. The hole deepened and still deepened. At last Tom said, "It ain't any use, Huck, we're wrong again."

Huck dropped his shovel. "That's it," said he. "We

got to give this one up. Besides this kind of thing's too awful, here this time of night with witches and ghosts a-fluttering around so. I feel as if something's behind me all the time; and I'm afeared to turn around, becuz maybe there's others in front a-waiting for a chance. I been creeping all over, ever since I got here."

"Well, I've been pretty much so, too, Huck."

"Say, Tom, let's give this place up, and try somewheres else."

"All right, I reckon we better. The haunted house. That's it!"

"Blame it, I don't like haunted houses, Tom. And you know mighty well people don't go about that haunted house in the day nor the night."

"But ghosts don't come around in the daytime, so what's the use of our being afeared?"

"Well, all right. We'll tackle the haunted house if you say so—but I reckon it's taking chances."

They had started down the hill by this time and took their way homeward through the woods.

About noon the next day the boys arrived at the dead tree; they had come for their tools. When they reached the haunted house there was something so weird about the dead silence, that they were afraid, for a moment, to venture in. Then they crept to the door and took a peep. They saw a weed-grown, floorless room, an ancient fireplace, empty windows, a ruinous staircase; and here, there, and everywhere hung cobwebs. They entered, talking in whispers. They wanted to look upstairs. They threw their tools

For a moment they were afraid to venture in.

into a corner and made the climb. Up there were the same signs of decay. They were about to go down and begin work when—

"Sh!" said Tom.

"What is it?" whispered Huck.

"They're coming right toward the door."

The boys stretched themselves upon the floor with their eyes to knotholes in the planking.

Two men entered the house. Each boy said to himself, "There's the old deaf-and-dumb Spaniard that's been about town lately—never saw t'other man before."

"T'other" man was a ragged creature, with nothing very pleasant in his face. The Spaniard was wrapped in a serape; he had bushy white whiskers; long white hair flowed from under his sombrero. When they came in, "t'other" was talking in a low voice. "No," said he, "it's dangerous."

"Dangerous!" grunted the "deaf-and-dumb" Spaniard—to the vast surprise of the boys. "Coward!"

The voice made the boys gasp and quake. It was Injun Joe's!

The two men got out some food and made a lunch. Injun Joe said, "Look here, lad—you go back up the river where you belong. I'll take the chances on dropping into this town just once more. We'll do that 'dangerous' job after I've spied around a little. Then for Texas! We'll leg it together!"

"All right." Both men fell to yawning, and Injun Joe said, "I'm dead for sleep! It's your turn to watch."

Soon enough, however, both men began to snore.

The boys drew a long, grateful breath. Tom whispered: "Now's our chance—come!"

Huck said, "I can't—I'd die if they was to wake."

Tom urged—Huck held back. At last Tom rose slowly and softly, and started alone. But the first step he made wrung such a hideous creak from the crazy floor that he sank down almost dead with fright.

Now one snore ceased. Injun Joe sat up, stared around—smiled grimly upon his comrade, whose head was drooping upon his knees—stirred him up with his foot and said, "You're a watchman, ain't you! All right, though—nothing's happened."

"My! have I been asleep?"

"Oh, partly. It's sunset, nearly time for us to be moving, pard. What'll we do with what little dough we've got left?"

The coins were gold!

"I don't know—leave it here as we've always done, I reckon. No use to take it away till we start south. Six hundred in silver's something to carry."

"Well—all right—it won't matter to come here once more. We'll just bury it."

"Good idea."

The boys forgot all their fears, all their miseries in an instant. With gloating eyes they watched every movement. Luck! Six hundred dollars was money enough to make half a dozen boys rich! Here was the best sort of treasure hunting—they would not be wondering where to dig!

As Joe dug with his knife, it struck upon something.

"Hello!" said he.

"What is it?" said his comrade.

"It's a box, I believe." He reached his hand in through a hole in the wooden plank and drew it out—"Man, it's money!"

The two men examined the handful of coins. They were gold!

Joe's comrade said, "We'll make quick work of getting the rest of the box out. There's an old rusty pick over in the corner." He ran and brought the boys' pick and shovel. Injun Joe took the pick and unearthed the box.

"Pard," said Injun Joe, "there's thousands of dollars here."

"What'll we do with this—bury it again?"

"Yes."

At this answer Tom and Huck were delighted.

Then Injun Joe declared, "No! by the great sachem, no! I'd nearly forgot. That pick had fresh earth on it. What business has a pick and shovel here? Who brought them here—and where are they gone? What! bury it again and leave them to come and see the ground disturbed? Not exactly. We'll take it to my den."

"Why, of course! You mean Number One?"

"No—Number Two—under the cross. The other place is bad—too common."

"All right. It's nearly dark enough to start."

Injun Joe got up and went about from window to window peeping out. Then he said, "Who could have brought those tools here? Do you reckon they can be upstairs?"

The boys' breath left them. Injun Joe put his hand

Injun Joe turned toward the stairway.

on his knife and then turned toward the stairway. The steps came creaking up the stairs—when there was a crash of rotten timbers and Injun Joe landed on the ground amid the debris of the ruined stairway.

"Now what's the use of that?" said his comrade. "If it's anybody, and they're up there, let them *stay* there—who cares? If they want to jump down now, who objects? It will be dark in fifteen minutes—and then let them follow us if they want to. In my opinion, whoever left those tools in here caught a sight of us and took us for ghosts or devils or something. I'll bet they're running yet."

Joe grumbled awhile; then he agreed with his friend that they ought to get ready to leave. Shortly afterward they slipped out of the house and moved toward the river with their precious box.

Tom and Huck rose up, weak, and stared after them through the chinks between the logs of the house. Follow? Not they. They were content to reach ground again without broken necks, and take the townward track over the hill.

7

The Cave

THE NEXT week Tom heard that Judge Thatcher's family had come back to town. Both Injun Joe and the treasure sank into secondary importance for a moment, and Becky took the chief place in the boy's interest. He saw her, and they had an exhausting good time playing with a crowd of their schoolmates. The day was crowned in a fine way: Becky managed to get her mother to name the next day, a Saturday, as a picnic for all her friends.

By eleven o'clock the next morning a giddy company were gathered at Judge Thatcher's, and everything was ready for a start. The children were escorted by young ladies of eighteen and a few young gentlemen. The old steam ferryboat was chartered for the occasion. Sid was sick and had to miss the fun; Mary remained at home to entertain him.

Three miles below town the ferryboat stopped at the mouth of a woody hollow and tied up. The crowd swarmed ashore and soon there were shouts and laughter. After the feast there was a time of resting and chatting in the shade of the spreading oaks. By and by somebody shouted: "Who's ready for the cave?"

Everybody was. Bundles of candles were passed around, and right away there was a general scamper up the hill. The mouth of the cave was up the hillside—an opening shaped like the letter A. Its massive oaken door stood unbarred. Within was a small chamber, chilly as an icehouse, and walled by nature with solid limestone that was dewy with a cold sweat.

It was romantic and mysterious to stand here in the deep gloom and look out upon the green valley shining in the sun. But then the romping began again. The procession of children and young men and women went filing down the steep descent of the main path, the flickering candle lights dimly revealing the lofty walls of rock. McDougal's Cave was a vast labyrinth, a maze of crooked aisles that ran into each other and out again and led nowhere. It was said one might wander days and nights through its tangle of pathways and never find the end of the cave; and that one might go down and down, and still down, into the earth, and it was just the same—maze underneath maze.

The parade moved along the main path some three-quarters of a mile, and then groups and couples began to slip aside into branch avenues. By and by one group after another came straggling back to the mouth of the cave, panting, entirely delighted with the success of the day. They were astonished to find that they had been taking no note of time and that night was about at hand. The ferryboat with her wild passengers pushed into the stream and headed for home.

Becky and Tom wandered into the depths of the cave.

Meanwhile, Tom and Becky had been left behind.
They had visited the familiar wonders of the cave
with the rest of the company. Then the hide-and-seek
had begun, and Tom and Becky had played along
until they got tired of it and wandered down a curving
path. They held their candles up and read the web-

The bats chased the children a good distance.

work of names, dates, and mottoes with which the rock walls had been stained with candle smoke. Still drifting along and talking, they scarcely noticed that they were now in a part of the cave whose walls were not decorated with personal marks. They smoked their own names under an overhanging shelf and moved on. Soon they came to a place where a little stream of water trickled over a ledge. They found a steep natural stairway behind it. They made a smoke mark for their future guidance, and started upon their quest to explore further into the cave. They wound this way and that, far down into the secret depths of the cave, made another mark, and branched off in search of novelties to tell the others about.

They came to a spring in the midst of a cavern, whose walls were supported by many fantastic pillars which had been formed by the joining of great stalactites and stalagmites, the result of the ceaseless water-drip of centuries. Under the roof vast knots of bats had packed themselves together, thousands in a bunch; the lights disturbed the creatures, and they came flocking down by hundreds, squeaking and darting at the candles. Tom seized Becky's hand and hurried her into the first corridor they found; and none too soon, for a bat struck Becky's light out with its wing while she was passing out of the cavern. The bats chased the children a good distance; but Tom and Becky plunged into every new passage they found and at last got rid of the perilous things. Tom found an underground lake, shortly, and they sat down by it and rested awhile.

Becky said, "It seems ever so long since I heard any of the others."

"Come to think, Becky, we are away down below them—and I don't know how far away north, or south, or east, or whichever way it is. We couldn't hear them here."

"I wonder how long we've been down here, Tom. We better start back."

"Yes, I reckon we better. But if the bats put both our candles out it will be an awful fix. Let's try some other way, so as not to go through there."

"Well, I hope we won't get lost."

But indeed they did get hopelessly lost.

They were finally so weary with hiking through the tunnels and along the underground paths that they lay down and slept. When they woke they walked further and drank some spring water. They were down to their last candle.

Becky said, "They'll miss us and hunt for us!"

"Yes, they will! Certainly they will!"

The children fastened their eyes upon their bit of candle and watched it melt slowly away, and then— the horror of utter darkness!

Both held their breath and listened. There was a sound like the faintest, far-off shout. Instantly Tom answered it, and, leading Becky by the hand, started groping down the corridor in its direction. Soon he listened again; again the sound was heard a little nearer.

"It's them!" said Tom. "They're coming! Becky, we're all right now!"

Their joy was almost overwhelming. They had to move slowly, however, because pitfalls were common, and had to be watched for. They soon came to one and had to stop. It might be three feet deep, it might be a hundred—there was no passing it. The children groped their way back to the spring. The weary time

The hand was followed by the body it belonged to—Injun Joe's!

dragged on; they slept again and awoke famished. Tom believed it must be Tuesday by this time.

Now an idea struck him. There were some side passages near at hand. It would be better to explore some of these than bear the weight of the heavy time in idleness. He took a kite string from his pocket, tied it to a rock, and he and Becky started, Tom in the lead, unwinding the line as he groped along. At the end of twenty steps the corridor ended in a "jumping-off place." Tom got down on his knees and felt below, and then as far around the corner as he could reach with his hands. He made an effort to stretch yet a little farther to the right, and at that moment, not twenty yards away, a human hand, holding up a candle, appeared from behind a rock! Tom lifted up a glorious shout, and instantly that hand was followed by the body it belonged to—Injun Joe's. Tom could not move. He was happy the next moment to see Joe take to his heels and get himself out of sight. Tom wondered that Joe had not recognized his voice and come over and killed him for testifying against him in court. But the echoes must have disguised the voice. He was careful to keep from Becky what he had seen. He told her he had only shouted "for luck."

They waited and waited by the spring and had another long sleep. The children awoke tortured with a raging hunger. Tom believed that it must be Wednesday of Thursday or even Friday or Saturday now, and that the search had been given up. He proposed to explore another passage. He felt willing to risk Injun Joe and all other terrors. But Becky was very weak. She said she would wait now, where she was, and die—it would not be long. She told Tom to go with the kite line and explore if he chose.

8

Finding Treasure

TUESDAY AFTERNOON came and went. The village of St. Petersburg mourned for the lost children. Still no good news came from the cave. The majority of the searchers had given up the quest and gone back to their daily lives, saying it was plain the children could never be found. Mrs. Thatcher was very ill. Aunt Polly had drooped into a settled sadness, and her gray hair had turned almost white.

Away in the middle of the night a wild peal burst from the village bells, and in a moment the streets were swarming with half-dressed people who shouted, "They're found! They're found!" Tin pans and horns were added to the din, and the population moved toward the river and met the children coming in an open carriage drawn by shouting citizens. The village was lit up; nobody went back to bed; it was the greatest night the little town had ever seen.

Aunt Polly's happiness was complete, and Mrs. Thatcher's nearly so. It would be complete, however, as soon as the messenger to the cave should get the word to her husband. Tom lay upon a sofa and told the history of the wonderful adventure and closed with a description of how he left Becky and went on an exploring expedition; how he followed two paths

Aunt Polly drooped into a settled sadness.

as far as his kite string would reach; how he followed a third to the fullest stretch of the string, and was about to turn back when he glimpsed a far-off speck that looked like daylight; dropped the line and groped toward it, pushed his head and shoulders through a small hole and saw the broad Mississippi rolling by! And if it had only happened to be night he would not have seen that speck of daylight and would not have explored that passage any more! He told how he went back for Becky and broke the good news and how she almost died with joy when she had groped to where she actually saw the blue speck of daylight; how he pushed his way out at the hole and then helped her out; how they sat there and cried for gladness; how some men came along in a rowboat and Tom hailed them and told them their troubles; how the men didn't believe the wild tale at first,

"Because," they said, "you are five miles down the river below the valley the cave is in"—then took them aboard, rowed to a house, gave them supper, made them rest till two or three hours after dark, and then brought them home.

Before dawn, Judge Thatcher and the handful of searchers with him were tracked out, in the cave, and informed of the news.

About two weeks after Tom's rescue from the cave, he stopped to see Becky. The judge and some friends set Tom to talking, and someone asked him, as a joke, if he wouldn't like to go to the cave again. Tom said he thought he wouldn't mind it.

The judge said, "Well, there are others just like you, Tom. But we have taken care of that. Nobody will get lost in that cave any more."

"Why?"

"Because I had its big door covered with iron two weeks ago, and triple locked—and I've got the keys."

"Oh, judge, Injun Joe's in the cave!"

Within a few minutes the news had spread, and a dozen rowboats of men were on their way to Mc-Dougal's Cave, and the ferryboat, well filled with passengers, soon followed. Tom Sawyer was in the rowboat that brought Judge Thatcher.

When the cave door was unlocked, a sorrowful sight presented itself in the dim twilight of the place. Injun Joe lay stretched upon the ground, dead, with his face close to the crack of the door. Tom was touched, for he knew by his own experience how this wretch had suffered. His pity was moved, but never-

Injun Joe was buried near the mouth of the cave.

theless he felt a sense of relief and security, now, which showed him how huge a weight of dread had been lying upon him since the day he testified against this bloody-minded outcast.

Injun Joe was buried near the mouth of the cave; and people flocked there in boats and wagons from the towns and from all the farms and hamlets for seven miles around.

The morning after the funeral Tom took Huck to a private place to have an important talk.

"Huck, that treasure's in the cave!"

"Say it again, Tom."

"The money's in the cave!"

"Tom—honest, now—is it fun or true?"

"True, Huck—just as true as ever I was in my life. Will you go in there with me and help get it out?"

"I bet I will! I will if it's where we can blaze our way to it and not get lost."

"Huck, we can do that without the least bit of trouble in the world. There's a mighty short cut that they don't anybody but me know about. I'll take you right to it in a rowboat."

"Let's start right off, Tom."

"All right. We want some bread and meat, and our pipes, and a little bag or two, and two or three kite strings, and some of these newfangled things they call matches. I tell you, many's the time I wished I had some when I was in there before."

They borrowed a rowboat and got under way at once. When they were several miles down the river, Tom said, "Now you see this bluff here looks all alike all the way down from the cave—no houses, no woodyards, bushes all alike. But do you see that white place up yonder where there's been a landslide? Well, that's one of my marks. We'll get ashore now."

They landed.

"Now, Huck, where we're a-standing you could touch that hole I got out of with a fishing pole. See if you can find it."

Huck searched all the place about, and found nothing. Tom proudly marched into a thick clump of sumac bushes and said, "Here you are! Look at it, Huck! It's the snuggest hole in this country."

They entered the hole, Tom in the lead. They toiled their way to the farther end of the tunnel, then tied their kite strings to rocks and moved on. A few steps brought them to the spring. They went on and soon entered and followed Tom's other corridor until they reached the "jumping-off place." The candles showed that it was not really a cliff, but only a steep clay hill twenty or thirty feet high. Tom whispered: "Now I'll show you something, Huck."

He held his candle high and said, "Look as far around the corner as you can. Do you see that? There—on the big rock over yonder—done with candle-smoke."

"Tom, it's a *cross*!"

" *'Under the cross,'* hey? Right yonder's where I saw Injun Joe poke up his candle!"

Huck stared at the sign awhile, and then said with a shaky voice: "Tom, let's git out of here!"

"What! and leave the treasure?"

"Yes—leave it. Injun Joe's ghost is round about there, certain."

"No, it ain't, Huck, no, it ain't. It would haunt the place where he died—away out at the mouth of the cave—five miles from here."

"No, Tom, it wouldn't. It would hang around the money. I know the ways of ghosts, and so do you."

Tom began to fear that Huck was right. But soon an idea occurred to him: "Looky-here, Huck, what fools we're making of ourselves! Injun Joe's ghost ain't a-going to come around where there's a cross!"

"Tom, I didn't think of that. But that's so. It's luck for us, that cross is. I reckon we'll climb down there and have a hunt for that box."

They searched everywhere, and then sat down discouraged. By and by Tom said, "I bet you the money is under the rock. I'm going to dig in the clay."

"That ain't no bad notion, Tom!" said Huck.

"My, but we're rich, Tom!" Huck said.

Tom's knife was out at once, and he had not dug four inches before he struck wood.

"Hey, Huck!—do you hear that?"

Huck began to dig and scratch now. Some boards were soon uncovered and removed. They had hidden a natural hole which led under the rock. Tom got into this hole and held his candle as far under the rock as he could, but could not see to its bottom. He stooped and passed under the rock. He followed its winding course, first to the right, then to the left, Huck at his heels. Tom turned a short curve and exclaimed, "My goodness, Huck, looky-here!"

It was the treasure box, sure enough, occupying a snug little cavern, along with an empty gunpowder keg, a couple of guns in leather cases, two or three pairs of old moccasins, a leather belt, and some other rubbish well soaked with the water-drip.

"Got it at last!" said Huck. "My, but we're rich, Tom!"

"Huck, I always reckoned we'd get it. It's just too good to believe, but we have got it, sure!"

They transferred the money from the box into the bags they had brought along, and the boys took it up to the cross rock.

They soon came out into the clump of sumac bushes, looked carefully out, found the coast clear, and were soon lunching in the rowboat. As the sun dipped toward the horizon they pushed out and got under way. They landed back in the village shortly after dark.

"Now, Huck," said Tom, "we'll hide the money in the loft of the widow's woodshed, and I'll come up in the morning and we'll count it and divide it, and then we'll hunt up a place out in the woods for it where it will be safe."

But just as soon as they had hid the money, a Mr. Jones saw them coming out and asked them to come along with him to the Widow Douglas's drawing room.

The place was grandly lighted, and everybody that was of any importance in the village was there. The Thatchers were there, the Harpers, the Rogerses, Aunt Polly, Sid, Mary, the minister, the editor, and a great many more, and all dressed in their best. The widow received the boys as heartily as anyone could well receive two such looking beings. They were covered with clay and candle grease. Aunt Polly blushed and frowned and shook her head at Tom.

Mr. Jones said, "I just brought them along in a hurry."

"And you did just right," said the widow. "Come with me, boys."

She took them to a bedroom and said, "Now wash and dress yourselves. Here are two new suits of clothes—shirts, socks, everything complete. Get into them. We'll wait—come down when you are slicked up enough."

After the widow had left the room, Huck said, "Tom, we can go out the window and down the slope of the roof. It ain't high from the ground."

"Shucks, what do you want to do that for?"

"Well, I ain't used to that kind of crowd. I can't stand it. I ain't going down there, Tom."

"Oh, bother! It ain't anything. I don't mind it a bit. I'll take care of you."

Some minutes later the widow's guests were at the supper table, and a dozen children propped up at little side tables in the same room, after the fashion of that country and that day. The widow now announced that she meant to give Huck a home under her roof and have him educated; and that when she could spare the money she would start him in business.

Tom's chance was come. He said, "Huck don't need it. Huck's rich. Maybe you don't believe it, but he's got lots of it. Oh, you needn't smile—I reckon I can show you. You just wait a minute."

Tom ran out of doors. The company looked at each other and at Huck, who was tongue-tied.

"Sid, what ails Tom?" said Aunt Polly. "He—well, there ain't ever any making of that boy out. I never—"

Tom entered, struggling with the weight of his sacks, and Aunt Polly did not finish her sentence. Tom poured the mass of yellow coin upon the table and said, "There—what did I tell you? Half of it's Huck's and half of it's mine!"

The spectacle took the general breath away. All gazed, nobody spoke for a moment. Then there was a call for an explanation. Tom's tale was long, but brimful of interest.

The money was counted. The sum amounted to a little over twelve thousand dollars. It was more than anyone present had ever seen at one time before.

The reader may rest satisfied that Tom and Huck's windfall made a mighty stir in the poor little village of St. Petersburg. So vast a sum, all in actual cash, seemed next to incredible. It was talked about, glorified, until every "haunted" house in St. Petersburg and the neighboring villages was pulled apart, plank by plank, and its foundations dug up and ransacked for hidden treasure—and not by boys, but men. Wherever Tom and Huck appeared they were admired, stared at. The village paper published stories of the boys' lives.

The Widow Douglas put Huck's money into a bank account, and Judge Thatcher did the same with Tom's at Aunt Polly's request. Each lad had an income, now, that was simply huge—a dollar for every weekday in

Judge Thatcher hoped to see Tom a soldier someday.

the year and half of the Sundays. A dollar and a quarter a week would board, lodge, and school a boy in those old simple days—and clothe him and wash him, too, for that matter.

Judge Thatcher had a great opinion, now, of Tom. He said that no commonplace boy would ever have got his daughter out of the cave. The judge hoped to see Tom a great lawyer or a great soldier someday. He said he meant to look to it that Tom should be

Huck was kept clean, neat, brushed and combed.

admitted to the National Military Academy and afterward trained in the best law school in the country, in order that he might be ready for either career or both.

Huck Finn's wealth and the fact that he was now under the Widow Douglas's protection introduced him into society—no, dragged him into it, hurled him into it—and his sufferings were almost more than he could bear. The widow's servants kept him clean and neat, combed and brushed, and they bedded him

nightly in fresh sheets. He had to eat with knife and
fork; he had to use napkin, cup, and plate; he had to
learn his book; he had to go to church; he had to talk
so properly that his speech was becoming boring in
his mouth.

He bravely bore his miseries three weeks, and then
one day turned up missing. For forty-eight hours the
widow hunted for him everywhere in great distress.
Early the third morning Tom Sawyer wisely went
poking among the old empty barrels down behind the
abandoned slaughterhouse, and in one of them he
found Huck. He had slept there; he had just break-
fasted upon some stolen odds and ends of food, and
was lying down, now, in comfort, with his pipe. He
was dirty, uncombed, and wearing the same old rags
that had made him so interesting to look at in the
days when he was free and happy. Tom told him the
trouble he had been causing, and urged him to go
home. Huck's face turned sad. He said:

"Don't talk about it, Tom. I've tried it, and it don't
work; it don't work, Tom. It ain't for me; I ain't used to
it. The widder's good to me, and friendly; but I can't
stand them ways. She makes me git up just at the
same time every morning; she makes me wash, they
comb me all to thunder; she won't let me sleep in the
woodshed; I got to wear them blamed clothes that
just smothers me, Tom; they don't seem to let any air
git through 'em, somehow; and they're so rotten nice
that I can't set down, nor lay down, nor roll around
anywher's; I hain't slid on a cellar door for—well it
'pears to be years; I got to go to church and sweat

and sweat—I hate them ornery sermons! I can't ketch a fly in there, I can't chaw. I got to wear shoes all Sunday. The widder eats by a bell; she goes to bed by a bell; she gits up by a bell—everything's so awful reg'lar a body can't stand it."

"Well, everybody does that way, Huck."

"Tom, it don't make no difference. I ain't everybody, and I can't *stand* it. It's awful to be tied up so. And grub comes too easy—I don't take no interest in vittles that way. I got to ask to go a-fishing; I got to ask to go in a-swimming—derned if I hain't got to ask to do everything. Well, I'd got to talk so nice it wasn't no comfort—I'd got to go up in the attic and rip out awhile, every day, to git a taste in my mouth, or I'd 'a' died, Tom. The widder wouldn't let me smoke; she wouldn't let me yell, she wouldn't let me scratch before folks. And, dad fetch it, she prayed all the time! I never see such a woman! I *had* to shove off—I just had to. And, besides, that school's going to open, and I'd 'a' had to go to it—well, I wouldn't stand *that*. Looky-here, Tom, being rich ain't what it's cracked up to be. It's just worry and worry, and sweat and sweat, and a-wishing you was dead all the time. I wouldn't ever got into all this trouble if it hadn't 'a' been for all that money; now you just take my sheer of it along with yourn, and gimme a ten-center sometimes—not many times, becuz I don't give a dern for a thing without it's tollable hard to git—and you go and beg off for me with the widder."

"Oh, Huck, you know I can't do that. 'Tain't fair. And, besides, if you'll try this thing just a while longer you'll come to like it."

"I'll smoke private and cuss private," Huck promised.

"Like it! Yes—the way I'd like a hot stove if I was to set on it long enough. No, Tom, I won't be rich, and I won't live in them cussed smothery houses. I like the woods, and the river, and the barrels, and I'll stick to 'em, too. Blame it all!"

"But, Huck, we can't let you into the gang if you ain't respectable, you know."

Huck's joy disappeared. "Can't let me in, Tom? You wouldn't shet me out, would you, Tom? You wouldn't do that, now, *would* you, Tom?"

"Huck, I wouldn't want to, and I *don't* want to—but what would people say? Why, they'd say, 'Mf! Tom Sawyer's Gang! pretty low characters in it!' They'd mean you, Huck. You wouldn't like that, and I wouldn't."

Huck was silent for a time. Finally he said, "Well,

I'll go back to the widder for a month and tackle it and see if I can come to stand it, if you'll let me b'long to the gang, Tom."

"All right, Huck, it's a whiz! Come along, old chap, and I'll ask the widow to let up on you a little."

"Will you, Tom—now will you? That's good. If she'll let up on some of the roughest things, I'll smoke private and cuss private, and crowd through or bust. When you going to start the gang?"

"Oh, right off. We'll get the boys together and have the initiation tonight, maybe."

"Have the which?"

"Have the initiation."

"What's that?"

"It's to swear to stand by one another, and never tell the gang's secrets."

"That's fine—that's mighty fine, Tom, I tell you."

"Well, I bet it is. And all that swearing's got to be done at midnight, in the lonesomest, awfullest place you can find—a haunted house is the best, but they're all ripped up now."

"Well, midnight's good, anyway, Tom."

"Yes, so it is. And you've got to swear on a coffin, and sign it in blood."

"Now, that's something like! Why, it's a million times bullier than pirating. I'll stick to the widder till I rot, Tom; and if I git to be a reg'lar ripper of a robber, and everybody talking 'bout it, I reckon she'll be proud she brought me in out of the wet."